PORKER
FINDS A CHAIR

by Sven Nordqvist

Carolrhoda Books, Inc./Minneapolis

Every day Porker goes for a walk. Today Porker is looking for raspberries. Instead of raspberries, though, Porker finds something he has never seen before. He stops, looks, and wonders — what is that strange thing that's lying there?

I've never seen anything like this before. I wonder where it came from. I wonder if more are coming. Porker looks around. There are no more coming.

These are just right for holding on to, Porker thinks as he grabs the strange thing. Perhaps I'm supposed to stand on the two sticks below. Help, it's falling over!

Uh-oh. I'd better put it back the way it was. At least I can hang my cap on it. And so he does.

Soon a jolly man walking many dogs comes by.

"Can you, kind sir with so many dogs, tell me what this is?" Porker asks.

"That's a chair, of course," says the jolly man.

"A chair? What's a chair?"

"You must know what a chair is. A chair is used to sit on, to lean your back against, so you don't have to sit on the ground. Ha ha ha, what's a chair?" The jolly man laughs and goes on his way.

A chair to sit on and lean your back against? I've never heard of such a thing. I just sit on the ground or at best on a stump, thinks Porker. He sits on the chair.

Then Speedway comes along on his racing bike.

"Hi, Speedway, I've found a chair," says Porker. "I can lean my back against it and hang my cap on it. You can hang your cap on it, too."

"Ha ha ha," laughs Speedway, "you're sitting on that chair back to front and upside down. You can't sit that way—turn the chair around! You're so silly, Porker." Speedway steps on the gas and races away.

"I'm not silly," Porker mutters, "I've just never seen a chair before." He turns the chair around. This is the right way to sit on a chair, Porker decides. The chair is quite steady now. As a matter of fact, it *is* better like this.

It even stays on when I walk. It's a bring-with-you chair. This will be great when I go to a party and it says "bring your own chair" on the invitation. I'll be able to carry a present in one hand and a flower in the other.

Along comes Dragonfly whirling down the road, spinning and fluttering and giggling.

"Hello, Dragonfly," shouts Porker joyfully. "I've just found a bring-with-you chair. I can take it to parties. It's a very fine chair — quite comfortable. Only after a while it gets a little uncomfortable."

"Hee hee hee, how silly you are, Porker," giggles Dragonfly. "You don't even know how to sit on a chair. You have a perfectly ordinary chair, but it's upside down."

"The legs aren't supposed to be up in the air — no, no — the chair's back is up and its legs are down. And you sit on the seat, not on the ground. You lean your back against the back, understand? Like this! Hee hee hee." Twitter and giggle and presto, she's gone.

Porker tips over. Lying on the ground he thinks, Dragonfly is always laughing at me, but she's usually right. I wonder, did she mean like this? It doesn't feel right to sit like this. Dragonfly explains things in such a scatterbrained way — just dances and gabbles away.

A tall man with a radio sees Porker and stops.

"You sit in a strange way, my young man," he says. "Did you try to sit down from underneath and get stuck? Or did the chair attack you from behind?"

"It's a bring-with-you chair — a party chair, I think," says Porker. "I was quite pleased with it until Dragonfly came by and laughed at me. Now I don't know what to think."

"The chair should stand on all four legs with the back up, and you're supposed to sit on the other side of the seat," the man explains, pointing every which way.

Porker tries to follow the man's directions.

"What do you mean 'on all four legs'? I can't very well sit and stand at the same time, can I?"

The man chuckles. "The *chair* is supposed to stand on all four legs. *You* are supposed to sit on the seat. I've seen better sitters, Porker. You look silly."

"I am not silly," Porker says firmly. "I've just never seen a chair before."

"You've never seen a chair before? Then I'll demonstrate," says the man. "Stand the chair up and sit on it like this. Put the radio on your lap so you can hear it properly."

So Porker sits on the chair. I don't have a radio, Porker says to himself. At least I'm sitting just like the tall man sat. It feels fine, like sitting on a stump. The chair is steady, but my feet can't reach the ground. That's good — if the ground is wet. Otherwise, it's not so good. But how can I be sure that this is a chair and that this is the proper way to sit on a chair? And why should I have a radio on my lap?

Here comes a lady. I'll ask her if I'm doing this right, Porker thinks.

"Hello, lady. Do you think I'm sitting nicely on this chair?"

"Yes, yes, you do look great! Can you sit so nicely all by yourself? How very clever you are. Are you comfortable?"

"Oh yes, very comfortable. I don't have a radio, though."

"No, but you can wish for one."

You can't count on some people, thinks Porker. They think *everything* is just fine. I'd better ask someone else.

"Look how well I can sit on my stump!" Porker shouts. A man with lots of suspenders stops.

"That's not a stump, that's a chair," the man says sternly. "Sit properly! Behave yourself! Don't play with expensive chairs!"

This is obviously wrong, thinks Porker.

Porker stands the chair up and sits on it. This must be the proper way to sit on a chair. I'll ask one more time, just in case. "Hello, Fisherman. Do you see anything that looks peculiar?"

"No Porker, I don't."

"Here I am, sitting on a chair."

"I see that. Good-looking chair. Is it yours?"

"Yes. Am I sitting nicely?"

"You couldn't be sitting any better."

So this is how it should be, thinks Porker. This is a chair, and this is the proper way to sit on it. I don't need a radio. I don't need anything else, either. Now I know. I can go on my way, then.

I wonder — what is that strange
thing that's lying there?

Library of Congress Cataloging-in-Publication Data

Nordqvist, Sven.
    Porker finds a chair.

    Translation of: Nasse hittar en stol.
    Summary: Porker finds a chair but can't figure out
how to sit on it.
    [1. Bears — Fiction. 2. Chairs — Fiction]
I. Title.
PZ7.N7756Po   1989   [E]   88-35358
ISBN 0-87614-367-2 (lib. bdg.)

Manufactured in the United States of America

1   2   3   4   5   6   7   8   9   10   99   98   97   96   95   94   93   92   91   90   89

DATE DUE

NOV 2 9 '98			
2/10/02	ILL # 3579593 CIB		
SEP 2 0 2011			
GAYLORD			PRINTED IN U.S.A.